This book belongs to

Bluebell Glade

Dandelion Dell

Heart of Misty Wood

Hawthorn Hedgerows

How many Fairy Animals
books have you collected?

🌼 Chloe the Kitten
🌼 Bella the Bunny
🌼 Paddy the Puppy
🌼 Mia the Mouse

And there are more magical
adventures coming very soon!

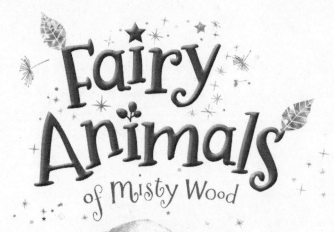

Fairy Animals
of Misty Wood

Paddy the Puppy

Lily Small

Henry Holt and Company
New York

With special thanks to Thea Bennett

Henry Holt and Company, LLC
Publishers since 1866
175 Fifth Avenue
New York, New York 10010
mackids.com

First published in the United States in 2015 by Henry Holt and Company, LLC.
Originally published in Great Britain in 2013 by Egmont UK Limited.

Library of Congress Cataloging-in-Publication Data
Small, Lily.
Paddy the puppy / Lily Small. — First American edition.
pages cm. — (Fairy animals of Misty Wood ; 3)
"Originally published in Great Britain in 2013 by Egmont UK Limited."
Summary: Paddy the Pollen Puppy is so excited about today being his
birthday that he causes all sorts of trouble. Includes activities.
ISBN 978-1-62779-143-4 (paperback) — ISBN 978-1-62779-362-9 (e-book)
[1. Fairies—Fiction. 2. Dogs—Fiction. 3. Animals—Infancy—Fiction.
4. Birthdays—Fiction.] I. Title.
PZ7.S6385Pad 2015   [Fic]—dc23   2014047288

Henry Holt books may be purchased for business or promotional use.
For information on bulk purchases, please contact the Macmillan Corporate
and Premium Sales Department at (800) 221-7945 x5442
or by e-mail at specialmarkets@macmillan.com.

First American Edition—2015
Printed in the United States of America by
R. R. Donnelley & Sons Company, Harrisonburg, Virginia

7 9 10 8 6

Contents

CHAPTER ONE

A Very Exciting Morning

The sun had just come out to play above Misty Wood. Golden light danced all over the fresh green leaves of the trees and warmed the

beautiful flowers in the valleys and meadows. Everything was bursting with color.

In a cozy den under the Hawthorn Hedgerows, sparkling sunbeams nudged the mossy bed of Paddy the Pollen Puppy. Paddy was curled up in a furry ball, but he wasn't asleep. He'd been awake for *ages*. Today was his birthday, and he'd woken up early because he was so excited!

Paddy gazed around the den

at his mom; his dad; and his sister,

Pippa. Their floppy ears were lying

over their front legs, and their eyes
were shut tight.

"Uhhh . . . hmmm," snored
Paddy's dad, his fluffy tail
twitching.

"Hmmm . . . uhhh," snored his
mom, her silky ears quivering.

Paddy sighed. "I wish they'd
wake up," he said to himself.

He got up and padded in
a circle on his cushion of moss.
Around and around and around.

Soon he felt dizzy, so he flopped
down again. He wriggled onto his
back and waved his white paws
in the air. Then he rolled over and
opened his glittery yellow wings.
He longed to fly across the den and
pounce on his mom's back, or give
his sister's tail a playful tug. But he
knew he shouldn't. They would be
grumpy if he woke them up early.

Like all the other fairy animals
in Misty Wood, Pollen Puppies had

an important job to do. They had to flick pollen around the meadows with their tails so that the flowers could grow. It was very busy work, so they needed plenty of sleep.

Paddy decided to think about his birthday party while he waited for everyone to wake up.

It's going to be the best party EVER, he thought. *There'll be hazelnut cake and elderflower juice and sticky chestnut buns, and we'll collect*

6

bubbles from Moonshine Pond and blow them all over the wood!

His tail began to wag at the very idea.

But, first of all, I'll have to open my presents. Paddy grinned, showing his velvety pink tongue. *I wonder what Mom and Dad got for me this year. . . .*

He looked around the den. His present must be hidden somewhere. His mom, dad, and sister were all

sleeping on comfy moss cushions
just like his. Maybe they'd slipped
his present underneath one of them?
But no—then it would get squashed.
It must be hidden somewhere else.

Paddy stretched his wings
and hopped off his cushion. He
checked the beautiful cobweb that
hung above the entrance to the
den. It had already been decorated
with sparkling dewdrops by the
Cobweb Kittens. But apart from

the dewdrops glistening like jewels in the sun, the cobweb was empty. There was still no sign of Paddy's present.

"It must be here *somewhere*," Paddy muttered.

He put his shiny pink nose in the air and sniffed. But he couldn't smell anything apart from the sweet scent of flowers drifting down from the hedgerows.

He peered under the four

red-and-white toadstools that the family sat on to eat their meals.

Nothing.

He nudged the pile of berries that he and Pippa played catch with.

Nothing there, either.

He peeped into the corner of the den where his dad liked to sit and chew sticks.

No. Not a thing!

Disappointed, Paddy wandered

back over to his cushion. As he

clambered onto it, he looked up.

And there, wedged into the bush

above his mom and dad and Pippa, was a very strange shape. Paddy stared at it. He was sure it hadn't been there before. His tail started wagging again.

It must be his present!

The mystery shape wasn't
too big, and it wasn't too small. It
wasn't exactly round, but it wasn't
square, either. Paddy started
panting with excitement, trying to
work out what it could be. Maybe
it was a soft, grassy brush to keep
his fur and wings tidy. Or maybe
it was a daisy-chain collar to wear
on special occasions—like birthday
parties. Or, best of all, maybe it
was a bone—a big, fat, juicy bone

that he could sit and chew on for
weeks!

Paddy was so excited he
wanted to jump up and down. He
was so excited he wanted to bounce
all around. He was so excited he
wanted to spread his shimmering
wings and buzz about like a Misty
Wood bee. He just couldn't lie on
his bed a moment longer. Paddy
did a forward roll off his cushion
and landed near his mom and dad.

Maybe if he got a little bit closer to the shape, he'd be able to sniff it . . . and then he might be able to guess what it was.

But the shape was hard to reach. It was sitting in the arch of a hawthorn branch that curved right over his mom and dad's bed. If he was going to get any closer to it, he'd have to climb up the branch, just a little bit. . . .

Paddy placed one paw on the

bottom of the branch. Then he hooked another paw a little higher.

CREEEEEAAAAK went the branch.

Oh no! thought Paddy.

But his mom and dad stayed asleep.

Paddy placed one of his front paws even higher still.

CREEEEEAAAAK went the branch.

Oh no! thought Paddy.

But his mom and dad still stayed asleep.

Breathing a sigh of relief, Paddy climbed even higher. Soon he'd be able to sniff the mysterious shape and find out what it was.

CREEEEEAAAAK went the branch.

Oh no! thought Paddy.

CRACK went the branch as it gave way.

Oh no! Oh no! Oh no! thought

17

Paddy as his paws slipped. He was so shocked he didn't even have time to flap his wings. Instead, he tumbled down and landed with a bump—right on top of his mom and dad!

CHAPTER TWO

Aaahhh-choo!

"Paddy!" his mom and dad cried as they leaped out of bed, their fur standing on end.

"Oops!" yelped Paddy. "Sorry, Mom! Sorry, Dad!"

Paddy's dad had been so startled that he'd jumped onto Pippa's mossy bed.

"Help! The sky's fallen on top of me!" Pippa cried, waving her silky paws in the air.

"Don't worry, Pippa," her mom said. "It's only Dad."

"But why has *Dad* fallen on top of me?" Pippa asked sleepily.

Paddy's dad scampered back to his own cushion. "Because

21

Paddy fell on top of *me*," he said.
"What were you doing, Paddy?
You've woken all of us up!"

Paddy covered his eyes with
his paws. "I didn't mean to," he
whimpered. "I just saw the shape
up in the bush and I . . . I . . .
thought it might be . . . might
be . . . my . . ."

Paddy had given everyone
such a shock that he didn't even
dare mention his birthday. He

peeped between his paws, hoping

they weren't too upset.

"Ah, of course!" His mom

smiled. "You thought it was your

present! Happy birthday, Paddy!"

Paddy's dad smoothed

down his brown-and-cream fur

and patted Paddy's head. "Don't worry, Paddy. It was time to get up anyway. Happy birthday!"

Pippa's eyes were wide open now, and she bounded down from her cushion to give Paddy a lick. "It's your birthday!" she woofed. "I don't mind being woken up for that!" Pippa fluttered her yellow wings and clapped her paws together. "Happy birthday, Paddy!"

Paddy grinned. He wasn't
in trouble after all! He glanced
up at the strange shape again.
"So . . . *is* that my present?" he
panted eagerly.

His mom laughed. "No, it
isn't. It's a bluebird's nest! And it's
a good job you didn't manage to
climb all the way up there, because
it's full of eggs that are almost
ready to hatch. Now, why don't we
have some birthday breakfast?"

While their mom prepared some poppy-seed bread with homemade blackberry jam, Pippa and Paddy fetched their wooden plates. They scrambled up onto their toadstools, and soon they were digging in.

"As soon as you've finished, you have to go and do your special job," Paddy's mom said.

"But it's my birthday!" replied Paddy. "Can't I just have fun today?"

26

His mom smiled. "Pollen
Puppies *always* have fun, no matter
what they're doing."

"Hmm, yes, that's true,"

27

said Paddy, thumping his tail in agreement.

"And you have to go," said his dad, "because we need to get your party ready for when you come back."

"Oooh!" Paddy's tail began to wag even harder. "In that case, we'll go right now!"

Paddy and Pippa skipped out of their den into the bright sunshine. They opened their

glistening wings and flitted up over the hedges.

It was a beautiful summer's day. Little clouds were drifting across the sky like wisps of cotton candy. Paddy twitched his shiny pink nose and smiled. He could smell the sweet scent of hawthorn blossoms and dusky pink roses.

Down below, one of their neighbors, Heidi the Holly Hamster, was nibbling the leaves of

29

a holly bush into shape. She had to start early, so they'd be ready for Christmas.

"Good morning, Heidi!" Paddy woofed. "It's my birthday!"

Heidi waved her tiny paw at him. "I know! Happy birthday, Paddy! See you at your party!"

Paddy and Pippa went on their way. They flew over fairy mushroom rings and a sea of nodding dandelion clocks, then

AAAHHH-CHOO!

floated down into Honeydew
Meadow. The flowers were in full
bloom—golden buttercups and
purple foxgloves, fiery red poppies
and soft, creamy lilies. They looked
wonderful, and they were all laden
with pollen. All they needed now
was a flick from a Pollen Puppy's
tail so that new flowers would grow!

When Paddy came in to
land, a crowd of puppies gathered
around him at once.

"Happy birthday!" they chorused. Then they turned up their noses and gave a happy, doggy howl. "Wahhooooooow!"

Paddy wanted to jump for joy.

The puppies set to work, bouncing through the meadow, wagging their tails. Paddy was so excited, his tail batted to and fro in a blur. His mom was right—his special job was fun! And it was more fun than ever on his birthday!

33

Flick . . . flick . . . flick . . .

Flickflickflick.

Flickety-flickflickflick . . .

Paddy had never wagged his tail so fast in his life!

And then he heard a noise.

"Aaahhh-choo!" sneezed his friend Petey, one of the other Pollen Puppies.

"Aaahhh . . . CHOO!" sneezed Polly, a pretty puppy with silky gray ears.

34

"AAAHHH . . . CHOO!
AAAHHH . . . CHOO!
AAAHHH . . . CHOO!"

Paddy looked around the meadow. His tail had flicked up clouds and clouds of pollen. All the other Pollen Puppies had stopped. Their sparkly wings were flat. Pippa was wiping her eyes with her paws. Others were spluttering and sneezing. Some were rubbing their little button

noses, trying to stop them from tickling.

"Paddy!" cried Petey. "You're working so fast that you've flicked ten times too much pollen! Aaahhh . . . choo!"

"Ooouuu!" howled Paddy in dismay. He looked back at his furry tail, which was still waving to and fro. "What do you think I should do?"

"We know you're excited about your birthday," a spotted puppy

named Pepper said. "So maybe you should use up some of your energy. Why don't you go flick pollen in Golden Meadow? Maybe by the time you've flown all the way there, your tail won't be wagging so hard."

"Oh yes," woofed Paddy. He shook his wings and did a little jig. "That's a great idea! Look out, Golden Meadow—the Birthday Pollen Puppy is coming your way!"

39

CHAPTER THREE

Happy Birthday to Me!

Paddy launched himself into the air. He waved good-bye to his friends in Honeydew Meadow and set off through the Heart of Misty

Wood. Paddy wanted to take the long way. It was lovely and cool among the trees. Paddy swooped around the towering tree trunks, practicing his flying skills.

"Happy birthday to me, happy birthday to meeeee!" he sang.

He zoomed up high to wag his tail at a woodpecker, who was peck-peck-pecking up in a tree. Then he flitted down to do a somersault over a rotting log.

41

He had just started humming his birthday tune again when he spotted a lovely big pile of leaves sitting under a beech tree. They looked *so* inviting! Paddy flew higher and hovered for a moment. "This will be fun!" he giggled to himself.

He pointed his shiny pink nose at the pile and began diving down. His wings whirred as they got faster and faster and faster. . . .

"Happy birthday, dear Paddy!" he warbled at the top of his voice as he skidded into the leaves at top speed. "Happy birthday to MEEEEEE!"

The leaves flew everywhere. Paddy rolled around in them, kicking his paws wildly. There were brown leaves, red leaves, yellow leaves, gold leaves. There were big leaves, small leaves, fat leaves, thin leaves.

43

"Oh, this is so much fun.

I'm having the best birthday ever!"

Paddy exclaimed as he flicked the leaves with his tail.

But then, suddenly, he heard a loud voice.

"HEY!"

Paddy jumped.

"HEY!" the voice called again, s ounding very angry.

Paddy looked around.

"Yes, YOU!"

Paddy brushed the leaves from his fur with his paws. Then he

45

plucked one leaf from between his wings. "Who is it?" he squeaked, feeling a teeny bit scared.

"It's Hattie the Hedgerow Hedgehog," said the voice. "And you've just spoiled my hard work!"

Oh, dear.

Oh dear, oh dear, oh dear!

All at once, Paddy understood why there had been such a big pile of leaves sitting in the middle of the wood. The Hedgerow Hedgehogs

had their own special job, just like all the other fairy animals in Misty Wood. They used their prickles to pick up leaves and keep the woods neat. Paddy clapped his paw to his mouth as Hattie fluttered out from behind the beech tree.

"I'm sorry," Paddy whimpered. "I didn't think the pile belonged to anyone."

Hattie landed on the ground in front of Paddy. Her prickles were

47

fluffed out in all directions, so she looked like a big spiky ball. She sighed. "What's your name, little Pollen Puppy?"

"I'm Paddy. And I'm really, truly sorry," whispered Paddy. He bent his head so that his ears drooped over his eyes. He even managed to stop wagging his tail, just to show how sorry he was.

"It took me all morning to get those cleaned up," Hattie said, looking sadly at the leaves. "And when I saw you messing them up— and singing a song while you did it—I thought you were ruining my

49

work on purpose." She rustled her rusty-brown wings and sniffed. "But you do look *very* sorry, I must say. What was that song you were singing?"

"Happy birthday," Paddy mumbled, "to—to me."

Hattie folded away her wings. "To you, eh?"

Paddy nodded his silky head. "Yes. You see, I was so excited about my birthday, and when I saw your

leaves I just thought they would be wonderful to play in," he explained. "I didn't mean to ruin anything, I really didn't. In fact, I'm on my way to do my own special job. Even though it's my birthday."

"I see." Hattie rubbed her chin with her delicate paw. Then she sighed. "Well, never mind. There aren't too many leaves at this time of year. I don't suppose it will take me long to tidy them up."

51

"Oh, but I can help you!" Paddy barked. He allowed his tail to give a little wag. "I have so much energy because it's my birthday, I have to use some of it up before I get to Golden Meadow. Otherwise I'll flick too much pollen and make all the other Pollen Puppies sneeze again!"

Hattie looked surprised. "That's nice of you." She smiled. "And it would be fun to have

someone to work with today. I'm all on my own in this part of the wood."

"Really?" said Paddy. "Come on, then, let's get started."

Paddy watched as Hattie fluffed out her prickles. Then she curled herself into a ball and rolled along the ground so that her prickles picked up the leaves. She looked so funny covered in leaves that Paddy started to laugh.

"You look more like a *hedge*
than a hedge*hog*!" He giggled.

Hattie grinned. "That's how
I'm supposed to look!" she told him,
shaking the leaves into a pile.
"Come on, now. You try!"

Paddy rolled through the
leaves, then peered around to look

at his back. It hadn't worked. Not a
single leaf had stuck to his soft fur.

"Oh, dear," he said. "I suppose
I'll have to find another way to
help you."

"Try collecting them in your
mouth instead," Hattie suggested.

So Paddy scampered off and

picked up a mouthful of leaves. They felt so tickly against his tongue he had to try really hard not to laugh. He dropped the leaves on top of Hattie's and then went back for some more. He couldn't collect as many leaves in his mouth as Hattie could with her prickles, so he had to run to and fro, to and fro, his ears and wings flapping. It was hard work! But at last all of the leaves were in a neat pile again.

Hattie wiped her forehead with her paw. "Phew," she said. "We did it. Thank you, Paddy!"

"That's all right." Paddy grinned. "Now, I really must get to

Golden Meadow. But you'll come to my birthday party later, won't you? It's at Hawthorn Hedgerows."

"I'd love to!" said Hattie. "How exciting—a new friend and a birthday party, all in one day!"

CHAPTER FOUR

Where's My Breakfast?

With a last wave to Hattie, Paddy
flew out of the Heart of Misty Wood
and into the open lands beyond.
Soon, he was soaring over Dewdrop

59

Spring, where the Cobweb Kittens collected their dewdrops in the morning.

The water was twinkling in the sun. It looked so magical that Paddy couldn't resist fluttering toward the surface to trail his paws in the cool, clear water. Blue and pink dragonflies skimmed along beside him, while bright green frogs hopped jauntily across the lily pads. Then Paddy spotted something

else. Something that made him

think about his party. On the bank

of the lake, next to an old, gnarled

log, sat a little pile of acorns.

"Acorns!" Paddy cried. "The

best birthday parties *always* have
acorns!"

He flew down and landed next
to them. They were the biggest,
roundest acorns he'd ever seen.
He tried to remember the very
best games to play with acorns.
He loved *Hide the Acorn*, but he
couldn't play that on his own.
There was *Pass the Acorn*, but
that needed friends, too. Then he
remembered how one of the Bud

Bunnies had once shown him how to juggle. He imagined showing off to all his friends as they arrived at his party, juggling acorns high in the air.

"Up in the air, up in the air, juggle the acorns, if you dare!" he chanted.

Paddy grabbed a handful of acorns and began to throw them from one paw to another. But it was a lot harder to catch them than

he remembered. One of the acorns
flew up much too high. When it
came down again, it landed in
Dewdrop Spring with a big *PLOP!*

"Oh, dear," murmured Paddy.
"Never mind. There are still plenty
of acorns left."

He threw them up again.

"One, two, three, four, I'll catch
them with my tail and my nifty
paw!"

Paddy leaped around, trying to

catch the acorns. But as they came down, his paws got all tangled. *Thud! Bump!* went two of the acorns, landing on the bank and rolling into the water with a *plop*. As Paddy chased after them, a third acorn flew over his head and landed in the pond with a tinkly *splish*.

Then he heard a voice.

"Where's my breakfast?"

Paddy spun around. There,

PADDY THE PUPPY

sitting on the log, was a Stardust Squirrel. Usually, Paddy would have been very happy to see one. He loved Stardust Squirrels. Their fur glistened silver or dusky red, and they had delicate wings to match. When they shook their bushy tails, they sent showers of stardust all over Misty Wood. But this one wasn't shaking his tail. Instead, he was looking a little angry.

"B-b-b-breakfast?" stuttered Paddy.

"Yes." The squirrel nodded his silvery head. "I put a perfect pile of delicious acorns right next to this log. And now they're all gone!"

"Oh, dear," said Paddy, hanging his head in shame.

The squirrel looked at Paddy, tilting his head to one side. "I don't suppose you might know what happened to them?"

Paddy laid his wings flat along his back and tucked his tail between his legs. He felt terrible.

"I'm so sorry," he said sadly. "I didn't know they were your breakfast. It's my birthday, you see, and I'm so excited—I just thought I'd see if I could juggle them. I thought it might be a fun trick for my party, but . . ." He looked sadly toward the lake.

The Stardust Squirrel raised his tufty ears in disbelief. "You were trying to juggle?" he squeaked. "I've never seen a Pollen Puppy juggle."

"No, well, it's not what we do best," admitted Paddy.

"And what *do* you do best?"

Paddy cocked his head to one side. "Wag our tails."

"That's what I thought," said the Stardust Squirrel. Then he put

his paws to his mouth and started to shake.

Paddy stared. The squirrel was wobbling all over. Even his bushy tail had joined in. It was sending clouds of stardust into the air, covering everything with glitter.

Then Paddy realized what was happening. The squirrel was laughing!

"Haw haw haw haw!" the squirrel roared. "A Pollen Puppy

71

who thinks he can juggle! I've

never heard anything so funny in

the whole of Misty Wood!" Then

he stopped suddenly. "I'm sorry.

I don't mean to laugh at you—

especially on your birthday. It's just
that . . . that . . ."

He tried to make his face
serious, but he couldn't quite
manage it. His nose and whiskers
twitched, and his silver wings began
to wiggle again.

Paddy thought of how all the
acorns had plopped into the lake.
It must have looked very funny.
He began to giggle, too. Soon they
were both laughing so hard that

73

they rolled around together on the bank of the lake, jiggling their wings and clutching their sides.

At last, they sat up and wiped their eyes. The Stardust Squirrel had covered the whole bank with stardust.

"Thank you, Pollen Puppy," he said. "You might have lost my breakfast, but you've made me laugh. What's your name?"

"Paddy. What's yours?"

"I'm Sammy," replied the squirrel. "Now, I suppose I'd better go and find some more acorns."

"Oh, no," said Paddy, wagging his tail. "I should find them for you." He pointed back toward the Heart of Misty Wood. "There are lots of big oak trees just over there. Come on, I'll show you."

Together, they flexed their wings and flew off toward the giant oak trees. When they got there,

Paddy leaped and bounced around, sniffing out the plumpest, ripest acorns. Soon, Sammy had an even bigger pile than before!

"Thank you, Paddy!" said Sammy. "Looks like I've found a new friend as well as breakfast!"

"You're welcome," Paddy woofed. "Now, I'd better go and do my work in Golden Meadow. But will you come to my party later, at Hawthorn Hedgerows?"

Sammy twitched his bushy
tail, sprinkling stardust all over his
acorns. "Oh, yes please!" he cried.
"That would be great fun!"

CHAPTER FIVE

Paddy's Perfect Cushion

As Sammy started munching his breakfast, Paddy took off again for Golden Meadow, waving good-bye as he went. But his yellow wings began to feel heavy.

Flap ... flaaap ... flaaaap ...

Paddy was flying slower and slower. He'd woken up very early and it had been such a busy morning. Now he felt so tired that he was starting to sink toward the ground. "How will I ever reach Golden Meadow?" he yelped to himself.

Just below him, he saw a pretty hill covered in nodding buttercups. And right on top of the hill sat a

cushion. It was made of the softest, comfiest moss Paddy had ever seen, and it reminded him of his own snuggly bed.

Ooh, he thought. *That looks perfect for a nap. Just a quick nap . . .*

He floated down and flopped onto the cushion. He laid his head on the moss and closed his eyes. He was so tired that he fell asleep at once. And soon, he was dreaming.

It was a beautiful dream. He

was at the most wonderful birthday party in the world, and he was surrounded by presents. Everyone was cheering and clapping. The trees were decorated with daisy chains, and the air fizzed with stardust. Birds were twittering up in the branches, and all the fairy animals were singing birthday songs. Best of all, his mom and dad had given him the juiciest, tastiest bone he'd ever seen. Paddy was

dancing around it, wiggling his body and waggling his tail. Then all his Pollen Puppy friends linked paws with him and joined in.

But something wasn't right.

"Oh! What have you done?" he heard a squeaky voice say.

Paddy frowned. He tried to grab his lovely bone, but when his little jaws snapped shut, it disappeared!

Paddy began to panic. He

83

couldn't possibly lose his birthday bone. . . .

"I said, what have you DONE?" the voice squeaked again, louder this time.

Paddy jumped. His eyes popped open. And there, tapping him on the nose with a little paw, was a Moss Mouse. He had pure white fur, the finest blue-and-white wings . . . and a big frown on his tiny face.

"Oh!" yelped Paddy as he remembered where he was. "I was dreaming about a bone. A beautiful, juicy bone . . ." He rubbed his eyes sadly.

"I know." The Moss Mouse sniffed.

"You know? How?" Paddy cocked his ears in surprise.

"Look what you've done to my cushion!" The Moss Mouse started hopping up and down. "I'm

85

Magnifico the Moss Mouse, and I
pride myself on my moss cushions.
This one was as round and smooth
as a springtime moon. *Now* see
what shape it is!"

Paddy jumped off the cushion.
He stared. The Moss Mouse was
right. It wasn't round anymore.
The cushion was shaped like a
huge bone!

"My tail must have wagged
it into that shape while I was

dreaming," Paddy said, still staring at the cushion in disbelief.

"Yes!" exclaimed Magnifico, folding his front paws. "That's exactly what it did."

Paddy felt very upset. His overexcited tail was causing all sorts of problems today. Moss Mice worked so hard to make all the lovely moss cushions in Misty Wood. They got up at dawn to hunt out the fluffiest moss from the shadiest valleys and the deepest dells. Then they spent hours patting it into shape.

"I'm really sorry," Paddy said. "It's my birthday, you see, and I'm

88

so excited. It wasn't just any old bone that I was dreaming about. It was a *birthday* bone."

"Oh!" said Magnifico, twitching his tiny pink nose. "Well, that does make a difference."

"Does it?" Paddy pricked his ears hopefully. "You mean you're not mad anymore? I'll help you get the cushion back into its proper shape, I promise!"

"Hmm. Well, let's see."

Magnifico walked all around the cushion. He looked at it one way. Then he looked at it another way. With a blurry buzz of his blue-and-white wings, he clambered up onto it. He ran to one end of the cushion and peered off the edge. Then he scampered to the other end and peered off that side, too. Paddy watched him, holding his breath.

At last, Magnifico bounced

90

back over to sit in front of Paddy and began to chuckle.

"I think it's perfect," he said.

"Perfect?" Paddy wasn't sure he'd heard correctly.

"I've never had a cushion in the shape of a bone before," said Magnifico. "Especially not in the shape of a *birthday* bone. I'm going to keep it, just as it is—in your honor!"

"Oooooh!" exclaimed Paddy.

"Thank you! Will it stay here for a long time?"

"Of course," said Magnifico. He smoothed back his whiskers proudly.

"I told you. I only make the very best quality cushions."

"So, I could come here and sit on it any time I like?" Paddy panted.

"I don't see why not," said Magnifico. "What's your name?"

"I'm Paddy."

"We can name it, if you like." Magnifico paused for a second. "How about, *Paddy's Birthday Bone Cushion*?"

93

"Oh, yes, yes, yes!" Paddy yapped. "Thank you!" He jumped up and padded the cushion with his paws. He would come and have a nap here as often as he could. He opened his wings and flapped back down to sit next to Magnifico. "In return, will you please come to my birthday party later? It's at Hawthorn Hedgerows."

Magnifico's shiny eyes lit up. "You're having a party?"

94

Paddy nodded.

"A real one, not a dream one?"

"Yes." Paddy's tail began wagging wildly.

"Wonderful," sighed Magnifico. "I love parties."

"This one's going to be the best in the world," Paddy told him. "Even better than the one in my dream!" He glanced up and saw that the sun was now high in the sky. "Ooh, I'd better

95

go, or I'll never get all my work
done in Golden Meadow. See
you later, Magnifico—and thank
you again for my birthday
cushion!"

CHAPTER SIX

The Best Birthday Party Ever

Hovering over Golden Meadow

at last, Paddy was bursting with

happiness. The meadow's rainbow

colors shimmered in the sunshine, and he could just see the tips of other puppies' tails as they wagged their way around the swaying flower stems.

Paddy swooped down and landed softly. He was still excited, but he was careful to keep his tail much calmer now. *Flick . . . flick . . . flick . . .* it went. Pollen rose lightly and floated off on the gentle breeze, while other flowers opened their

petals wide to welcome it to a new home.

When half of the dandelion clocks had blown their seeds away, Paddy knew that it was time to go home. He had spread *lots* of pollen! He rose into the air and fluttered back toward Hawthorn Hedgerows.

What an amazing day I've had! he thought. He'd made three new friends—Hattie, Sammy, and Magnifico. He'd helped them tidy

leaves and collect acorns. He'd flicked more pollen than he'd ever thought a Pollen Puppy could. And he hadn't even had his birthday party yet! If only he didn't feel quite so tired . . .

As he floated down toward the hedgerows, Paddy's eyelids began to droop. He thought longingly of his little moss bed. Maybe he could have a snooze before all the fun began.

But then, just as he landed next to a purple toadstool, he heard a shout. A BIG shout.

"SURPRISE!"

Paddy peeped over the toadstool. Just ahead, in the clearing next to the hawthorn bushes, his whole family was waving and cheering. Pippa was bouncing up and down. And they weren't alone. All the other Pollen Puppies were there, and all his

friends from across Misty Wood.

There were Cobweb Kittens and

Holly Hamsters and Bud Bunnies

and even a couple of Moonbeam

Moles—and everyone knew that

moles preferred to go out in the

dark.

Then he heard a rustle of

rusty-brown wings.

His new friend Hattie the

Hedgerow Hedgehog was there!

Next, he saw a bushy silver tail,

which was sprinkling stardust
everywhere.

Sammy the Stardust Squirrel
was there!

Then he heard a cheeky squeak
at his feet. He looked down.

Magnifico the Moss Mouse
was there!

"Happy birthday, Paddy!"
everyone cried.

The glade had been decorated
just as Paddy had imagined in his

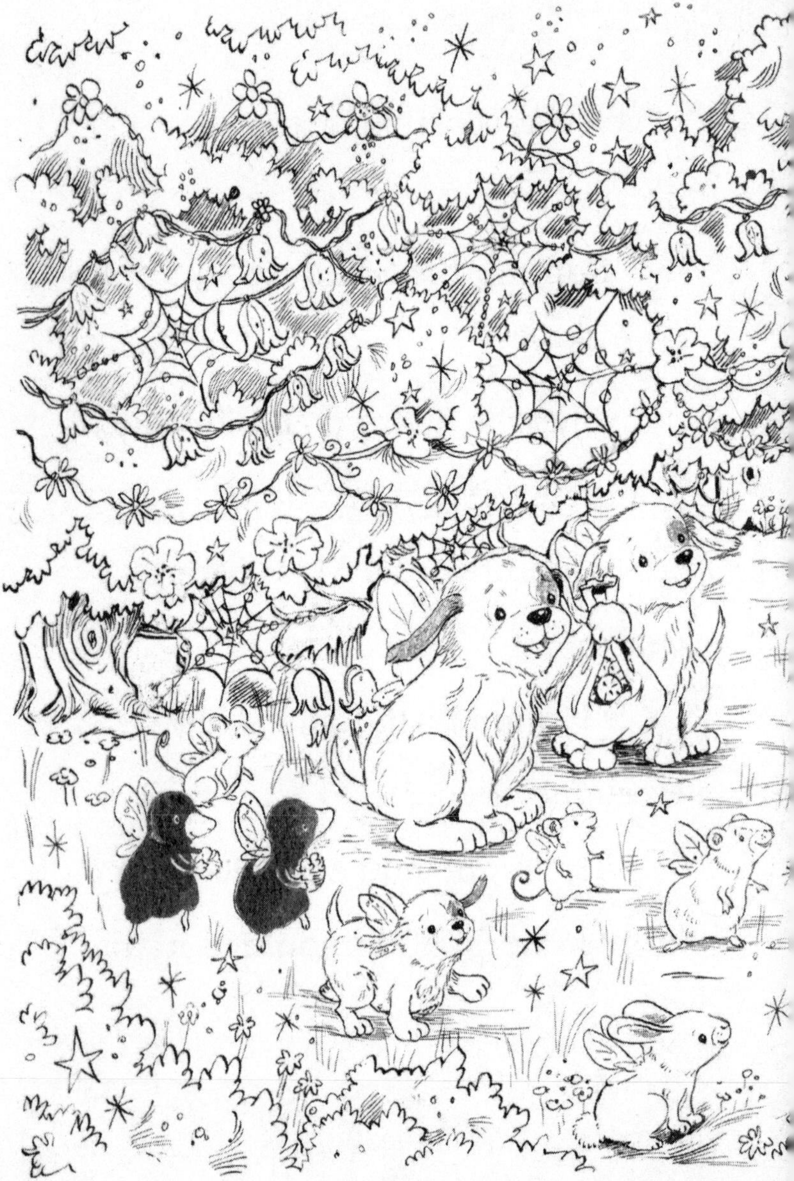

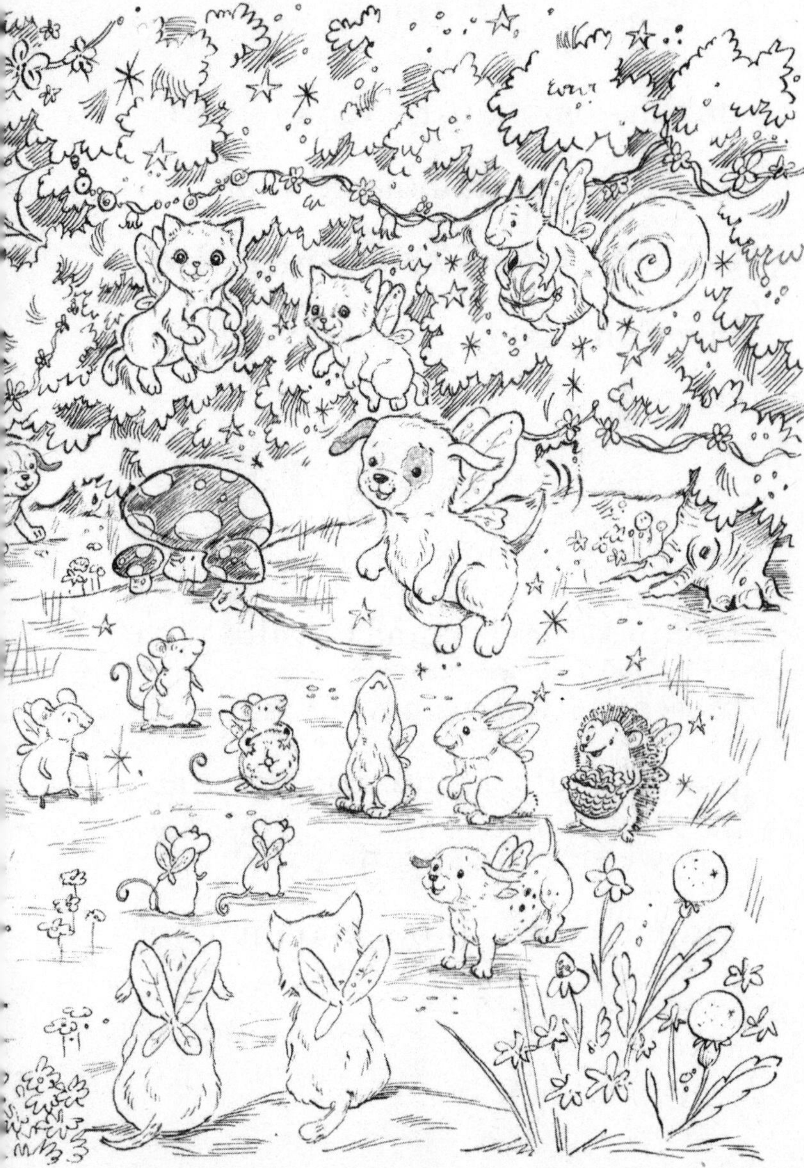

dream—only it was even prettier!
The cobwebs shimmered with
extra dewdrops, while garlands of
bluebells and poppies adorned all
the bushes.

The air filled with the sound
of fluttering fairy wings as
Paddy's friends came forward with
presents. Even his new friends had
brought gifts! Hattie had brought
a bowl made of sycamore leaves.
Magnifico had brought a miniature

moss cushion. And as for Sammy—
first he filled the glade with
shimmering stardust. Then, from
behind his back, he brought out a
whole parcel of conkers and acorns
to play with!

"Time for games, everyone!"
cried Paddy's dad.

Soon everyone had joined
hands and they all danced in a
circle, singing *Ring Around an Acorn*
at the tops of their voices. Then

they played *Conker Catch*, before

spreading out to play *Hide the Acorn*.

Paddy had never had so much fun!

At last, happy and weary, they

gathered for the birthday picnic.

Paddy's mom had spread out a

big mat made of pearly reeds from

Moonshine Pond, and it was laden

with treats and delicacies. Paddy's
eyes nearly popped out when he
saw everything! There were cowslip
tarts, daisy pies, fairy fancies,
and buttercup buns, along
with more honeysuckle fizz and
elderflower juice than even Paddy
could dream of.

But before they began to dig in, Paddy's dad came bounding out of their den with something else. Paddy's tail began to wag.

Would it be . . . ?

Could it be . . . ?

Paddy yelped happily as his dad handed him a gift wrapped in silvery leaves. As Paddy began to pull at it with his teeth, he was so excited that his whole body started to tremble.

Would it be . . . ?

Could it be . . . ?

One corner of the wrapping came open. Paddy sniffed with his pink button nose.

It *smelled* like a bone.

He tore some more of the leaves away.

It *looked* like a bone.

The last piece of wrapping dropped off, and Paddy bounced up and down with joy.

111

It WAS a bone!

And it was even juicier and tastier than the one he had seen in his dream.

"Thank you, thank you!"

Paddy barked, jumping around in circles.

Everyone clapped and cheered, then they began to eat and drink. Paddy gave his bone one lick, then decided to save it for later. There was so much delicious party food, he wanted to try it all. As he slurped honeysuckle fizz and chomped a daisy pie, he decided that this really was the best birthday party ever!

113

In the distance, the sun was dipping toward Sundown Hill. Golden rays played with the stardust in the air, while the shadows in the clearing grew longer.

Paddy thought there couldn't possibly be any more treats. He'd had so many! But his mom and dad had disappeared again, and all the fairy guests began to whisper behind their paws. Where had Paddy's parents gone? What were they up to?

Suddenly, there was a flurry of fur at the entrance to the family den. Paddy turned to look and saw his mom, dad, and Pippa holding a birthday cake between them. It was made of hazelnuts and rosehips, and it had a garland of ivy leaves tied in a bow around it. On the top, waving gently, were birthday dandelion clocks for Paddy to blow.

Everyone cheered again, and burst into song.

115

"Happy birthday, dear Paddy! Happy birthday to you!" they chorused.

"Happy birthday, dear Paddy! Happy birthday to meeeee!" Paddy sang along. His tail was wagging so fast, it nearly blew all the seeds from the dandelion clocks!

Just as the song came to an end, Paddy heard something else. Something tuneful and tinkly. It was coming from their den. . . .

116

Cheep!

Cheep cheep!

Cheep cheep cheep!

Paddy cocked his ears. "What is that?" he asked.

His mom smiled. "It's the bluebird chicks!" she told him. "They've just hatched. There are three of them—come and look!"

With a last burst of energy, Paddy bounded over to the nest. And there they were—three tiny

117

balls of fluff, each with a teeny beak, begging for food. And to think they'd hatched on his birthday. . . .

"They're the best present of *all*!" Paddy cried.

"Well, we're all happy that you've had such a lovely day." His mom smiled. "But don't forget to blow your birthday clocks!"

The birthday cake was sitting in the middle of the picnic. Paddy

THE BEST BIRTHDAY PARTY EVER

rushed back. As he filled his cheeks with air, he thought he was the luckiest Pollen Puppy in the whole of Misty Wood.

"One, two, three, *blow*!" chanted the crowd.

Paddy blew. The dandelion seeds flew up in a cloud, then floated off. Some of the guests laughed and chased after them.

But not Paddy. Paddy had finally run out of puff.

He lay down on his soft, mossy cushion and, with a happy sigh, he fell fast asleep.

Misty Wood Word Search

Can you find all these words from the story in this fun word search?

ACORN   GAME   TAIL
BONE   PARTY   WAG
DREAM   PRESENT
FLICK   PUPPY

```
E  A  C  O  R  N  O  E  O  H  S
B  E  H  V  S  G  A  M  E  N  N
O  P  F  H  N  I  E  H  P  S  R
N  E  D  I  S  T  T  A  R  R  E
E  P  I  S  O  H  H  E  E  S  I
D  R  W  A  G  Y  L  Y  S  T  T
R  L  A  H  T  P  I  C  E  S  E
E  U  E  R  S  F  M  I  N  A  D
A  A  S  Y  C  L  S  T  A  I  E
M  P  I  P  R  P  E  I  R  I  T
S  O  M  E  N  S  U  P  C  R  A
I  Y  O  R  W  G  R  P  A  K  I
F  E  M  H  L  I  H  F  P  R  L
N  R  T  P  A  C  E  E  V  Y  O
```

All about YOUR Birthday!

When is your birthday?

May 3

How old will you be on your
next birthday?

_9_

What present would you like?

a dog

What would you most like to do?

eat pizza

Which people would you like to be there?

family, friends and relitives

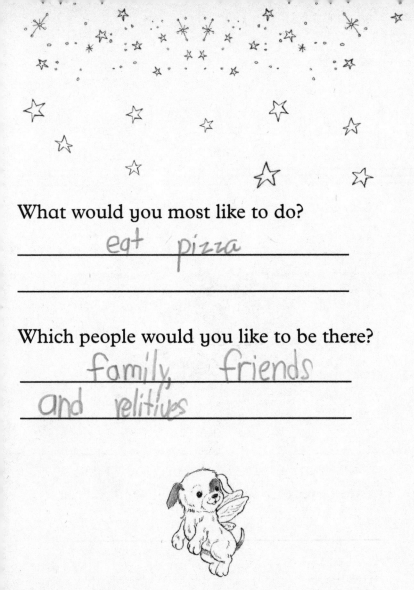

A Very Happy Birthday!

Paddy gets VERY excited about his birthday. What are your three favorite things about birthdays?

1. Presents
2. cake
3. friends

What other special occasions are really exciting?

1. Hannukah
2. Passover
3. St. Patricks day

Connect the Dots

Follow the numbers and connect all
the dots to make a lovely picture.
Start with dot number 1.

Can you guess what Paddy is holding?

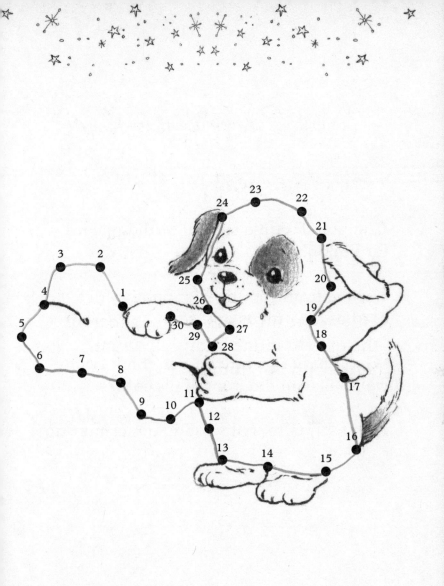

Make Paddy a Birthday Card!

Can you design a special birthday card for Paddy?

Use the frame on the next page. Make the card as colorful as you can!

What kind of picture do you think Paddy would like on the front of his card?

Don't forget to write Paddy a nice message!

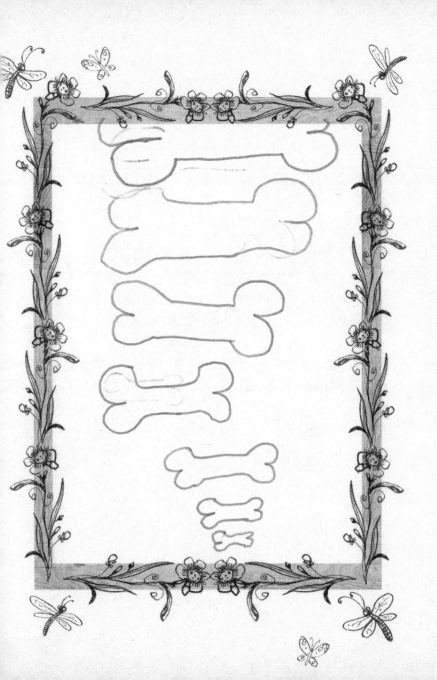

Fairy Animals
of Misty Wood

Meet more Fairy Animal friends!

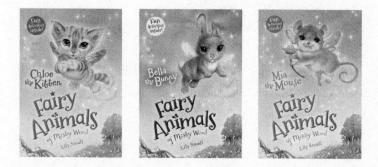